Fart Squad #5: Underpantsed!
Copyright   2016 by Full Fathom Five, LLC

Library of Congress Control Number: 2016942118
ISBN 978-0-06-236635-1 (trade bdg.) — ISBN 978-0-06-229053-3 (pbk.)

Design by Brenda E. Angelilli
16 17 18 19 20  CG/OPM  10 9 8 7 6 5 4 3 2 1
❖
First Edition

#5

# FART SQUAD

## UNDERPANTSED!

by **SEAMUS PILGER**
illustrated by **STEPHEN GILPIN**

**HARPER**
*An Imprint of HarperCollinsPublishers*

# CHAPTER ONE

Juan-Carlos Finkelstein was already late for school when the harsh reality of an empty dresser drawer stopped him in his tracks. "Mom!" he shrieked. "Where's my clean underwear?"

"I just bought a whole new bunch!" his mom called from downstairs. "Stop going through underwear so quickly!"

*You have no idea,* Juan-Carlos thought as he closed the empty drawer. That's when he noticed a pungent fartlike odor wafting over his dresser. He was pretty sure he hadn't farted all morning, and besides, he didn't recognize the smell as his brand. But he had more important things to concentrate on at the moment anyway, namely getting to school on time. So he turned his attention to his laundry hamper in the hopes of scrounging up a decent pair of boxers. When you're a superhero whose power comes from your superpowered farts, it tends to take a toll on your underwear collection.

A familiar voice from his clock radio made him pause. "Can you believe those kids?" a man asked. "Running around in masks, farting on everyone . . . I've heard of loving the smell of your *own* farts, but these kids must think other people love the smell as well!"

Juan-Carlos's father was a radio personality. He had his own morning show, *Shockin' Sheckey,* which he recorded live in his home studio, right in the Finkelstein basement. People either loved him or hated him—*or,* loved to hate him. Juan-Carlos, of course, thought his dad was a comedic genius. Even if he *was* picking on the Fart Squad right now.

But then his dad continued, "But seriously, folks, I'm just playing around. I actually think those kids are great! They really saved our butts— ha-ha!—with that whole itch- ing thing, and again with that dinosaur, and who knows what else.

They're stinking up the town—in the best possible way!"

*Dad's a fan!* Juan-Carlos thought happily. *Too bad I can't tell him that his son is one of those kids he's cheering for! Well, maybe someday.*

In the meantime, there was school to worry about. And that required clean clothes.

Pulling open the hamper, Juan-Carlos found two pairs of jeans, three T-shirts, five mismatched socks, and what looked like one of his dad's Grillmaster aprons. But no underwear.

*Oh well. Mom must have already grabbed them,* Juan-Carlos thought, peeling back the waistband of his pajama bottoms. "I'll have to wear these a second time."

Only, when he looked down, there was nothing between his pajama bottoms and himself.

"I'm sure I was wearing them when I went to bed," he muttered under his breath. "Maybe they came off during my sleep somehow?"

He wanted to ask his mother—maybe she'd taken them? But that didn't make any sense. Besides, even if she had, it wasn't like he could yell at her for doing his laundry. He'd just have to manage. She'd probably have a whole pile of clean underwear waiting when he got home.

By the time Juan-Carlos's bus arrived at school, he was in agony. Without underwear to

provide a protective layer, his jeans were rubbing him raw! He had to move really slowly as he stepped off the bus and carefully make his way up the stairs and into the building.

When he finally reached his classroom, Juan-Carlos gratefully slid into his assigned seat. Now that he was sitting down, he noticed that his classmates were also moving slowly. *They all look exactly how I feel,* Juan-Carlos thought. But there was no way his mom was washing all of *their* underwear, was there?

Clearly something else was going on here.

At lunchtime, Juan-Carlos sought out his friends: Darren Stonkadopolis, Walter Turnip, and Tina Heiney. They all winced every time they shifted in their seats.

"Let me guess," tiny Tina Heiney said as she looked around the table. "No underwear, right?"

"Nothing," Juan-Carlos admitted. "Even the dirty pair from last night is gone. And I don't know about you guys, but there was an awful fart smell coming from my dresser that most definitely did not come from me!"

"Same here!" Tina exclaimed. "Nothing like smelling other people's farts first thing in the morning to ruin your day." Tina might have had a dainty appearance, but she talked like a truck driver.

"And do you guys believe that my mom

actually accused me of throwing my under-wear in the garbage!" Darren said.

The other three all nodded as if on cue.

"Indeed," said Walter.

"Pretty much!" Tina answered.

"Sounds about right," said Juan-Carlos.

"I guess you guys have a point," Darren said with a sigh.

The truth is, throwing underwear in the garbage after one use is exactly the kind of thing Darren would do. He often acted without thinking, which got him in trouble at school, but made him the kind of quick-on-his-feet leader a team of superheroes like the Fart Squad needed.

"Did you know that your father referenced the undergarment situation this morning during his broadcast?" Walter commented to Juan-Carlos. "He joked that all of Buttz-ville had been drafted into special forces, because we're all 'going commando.'" When the others stared at him blankly, he explained, "Going commando means *going it alone*. As in, getting dressed without putting on any underwear."

Walter was as brainy as he was wide. He spent half the time explaining things to the rest of the Squad, and the other half of the time acting as their private blimp.

Tina rolled her eyes. "Guess we know where Juan-Carlos gets his sense of humor," she muttered.

Juan-Carlos brightened. "Really? Thanks!" That just made Tina roll her eyes again.

"It does seem that our current plight is widespread," Walter pointed out.

The four Squad members studied the crowd. One of the science teachers was tugging at her pants under the table, like she was trying to make them looser. And even their math teacher looked like she was in pain as she gingerly made her way across the cafeteria.

"Weird," Juan-Carlos agreed. After all, how did a whole school's underwear just disappear? And why?

"So what's the deal with everybody's underwear?" Juan-Carlos asked at dinner that night. "The kids at school said theirs were missing, too."

His mother shook her head. "I have no idea," she answered. "I've looked everywhere. Every pair in the house is just gone!"

"Maybe somebody needed them," Juan-Carlos's annoying little sister, Rivkah, piped up. "Maybe it was the Fart Squad!"

"Nonsense!" Mr. Finkelstein told her. He looked a lot like his son, only taller and with a bushy mustache that matched his slightly shaggy hair. "Why would they do something like that? Those kids are heroes—they'd never stoop to stealing people's underwear!"

Juan-Carlos nodded in agreement, but he felt his mood sink. It was nice to know his dad really did admire the Squad, even when he wasn't on the air. But at the same time, Juan-Carlos was a little frustrated. He looked up to his dad so much. But his dad, well . . . his dad rarely said anything that glowing about Juan-Carlos!

# CHAPTER TWO

The following evening, things got even worse.

"I went to the store to buy some new underwear," Juan-Carlos's mom told her family over dinner, "but there weren't any! Not a single pair! At first I thought maybe they'd just sold out, but then I heard one of the salesmen saying that all the underwear they'd had in stock had been stolen!"

"Stolen?" Juan-Carlos echoed.

"That's right." His mother wrinkled her nose. "And there was the most horrible smell in the store, too. It was awful!"

Juan-Carlos wondered if it was the same smell from his bedroom the previous morning.

Later that night, Juan-Carlos was watching TV with his family. "Tonight, breaking news," the *Buttzville Nightly News* anchor announced. "All of Buttzville's underwear has disappeared! Last night half the city reported missing underwear, and today the rest of the city called in with the same

complaint. Officials suspect the shadowy group known as the Fart Squad is to blame."

"Aw, what?" Juan-Carlos felt blindsided. "*Stealing?* The Fart Squad? That's not right!"

"Shush, we're trying to watch," his mom told him.

"Those guys are creepy," Rivkah chimed in. "And they smell!"

"Of course they smell—they're the *Fart* Squad," Juan-Carlos replied right before his mom shushed them both again.

"This quartet has been seen at the sites of several major events," the channel's lead reporter, Windy McGee, continued. "Including at recent UFO sightings and at the tar pit museum when the believed-to-be-extinct dinosaur Fartasaurus Rex went on a rampage through downtown. Now a terrible odor near the scene of the recent thefts seems to point to the foul-smelling foursome. Though nothing has been conclusively proven, authorities have said they are searching for these masked vigilantes and intend to question them regarding their whereabouts over the last few nights and whether they are involved in these recent thefts."

"That's crazy," Juan-Carlos muttered. "They're heroes, not villains. How can anyone not see that?"

"I couldn't agree more," his dad said. "Those kids are awesome! Imagine going around farting everywhere and people actually thanking you for it! Brilliant!" He chuckled. "I wish I'd thought of that! But all kidding aside, from everything I've heard, those kids have done nothing but try to help this town and its people. So the idea of them stealing underwear all of a sudden?" He winked at Juan-Carlos and tapped his nose. "It just doesn't smell right."

Juan-Carlos chuckled and said his good nights.

But as he slowly made his way up the stairs, he felt a tightness in his chest, which, when he thought about it, was kind of ridiculous. . . .

Was it even possible to be jealous of yourself?

# CHAPTER THREE

The next morning, on his way to school, Juan-Carlos learned that his family hadn't been the only ones to see the news the night before.

"It's those stupid kids," he overheard their mailman say to their neighbor Mrs. Kaffrey.

"They must destroy their own underwear all the time with those awful farts of theirs," Mrs. Kaffrey agreed, clutching her robe tighter around herself. "So now they're stealing ours!"

Juan-Carlos frowned. *Great! Now every-one thinks we're thieving criminals!*

As he climbed onto the school bus, the driver, Mr. Radek, was talking to the boy sitting in the front seat. "Darn kids," he muttered. "Stinking up the city and swiping underwear, too!" Juan-Carlos didn't know how much more he could take. Why was everyone against the Fart Squad?

"The Fart Squad didn't steal your underwear!" he burst out before he could stop himself. "They're heroes!"

Mr. Radek sniffed. "You don't know what you're talking about," he claimed. "It's got to be them. Who else could it be?"

"I wish I knew," Juan-Carlos muttered as he crept back toward his usual seat. All around him, kids shifted painfully as the bus lurched into motion.

Juan-Carlos observed the same trend later that day. "That Fart Squad is a menace," Juan-Carlos's teacher, Mrs. Andrews, said to herself as she sat down in her desk chair, wincing.

"The Fart Squad didn't do this!" Juan-Carlos insisted. "They help people!"

"More like they help themselves—to our underpants!" one of his classmates, Joey Fredericks, replied.

"It wasn't them!"

"Yeah?" another kid asked. "How would you know?"

"Oh, uh." Juan-Carlos sank down in his seat. "Just a feeling."

"Did you see the news?" Tina asked the rest of them that day at lunch. "They've decided we're the ones to blame for all this!"

"Yeah, I saw it," Darren said. "I just can't believe it."

"We *have* been on hand each time a crisis has occurred," Walter pointed out. "And thus it is not unreasonable to assume we might be responsible for their creation, rather than instrumental in their resolution. And unfortunate reports of a lingering stench aren't doing much to help our cause." He sighed. "It is disappointing, however. Not to mention frightening."

"Especially since they issued a warning to adults to keep a close eye on all kids," Tina added. "That's the last thing I need, my parents figuring out I'm on the Squad!"

They'd all heard the warning or seen it in the morning papers. With the police searching for the Fart Squad, parents were urged to keep track of their children and report anything suspicious.

Juan-Carlos shook his head. "My dad still believes in the Squad," he told the others. For once, he wasn't joking around. "Which means not everybody thinks we're bad. We can still fix this. We just have to figure out who's really behind it and get that underwear back!"

The others nodded. Yes, that would work— they could restore the town's underwear and

clear their names at the same time! "There's just one problem," Tina pointed out. "We have no idea who's taking the underwear!"

"Did you notice," Darren asked, "that the news said half the city's underwear disappeared the other night, and the rest of it went missing last night? So it took two days for whoever did this to cover the whole city."

"Indeed," Walter agreed. He pulled a newspaper out of his backpack and flipped to a page about the thefts, which showed a map of the city and had each area marked to show the night its underwear had disappeared.

The four friends studied the map. "It's like they split the city down the middle," Juan-Carlos pointed out. "We were all in the first half, here, and then they got the second half last night."

"Which means whoever did this probably started somewhere near the middle," Darren replied, "and they branched out in one direction the first night, then went the opposite way the second night." He traced a finger down the line separating the two halves. "Somewhere around here." At the center of town were warehouses and factories. South of that was city hall. North was their school—and where most of the town lived.

"I know someplace you could look,"

someone said behind them. The kids all turned. It was Janitor Stan, their friend and mentor! Stan often walked around during lunch, helping to keep the cafeteria clean and quiet, and now he stood beside their table. "It's the old Bottom factory," Stan continued. "Bottom's Bottoms. They made underwear—pretty much covered Buttz-ville's butts, if you know what I mean. But the company went bankrupt last year—bit of a scandal with the owner—and they closed the factory down."

"A scandal? What happened?" Darren asked.

Stan scratched his head. "I don't remember all the details, but there was something about cutting corners and a few workers getting hurt."

"Cutting corners? On underwear?" Juan-Carlos chuckled. "Wouldn't that just leave you with a hankie—or a diaper?"

"And the factory's still there?" Darren asked, ignoring Juan-Carlos's joke and pointing to the middle of the map.

"Sure, it's in the industrial sector, right near the river," Stan answered, indicating the very top of that line. "Can't miss it." He eyed the four of them. "If you're planning on going out there, just be careful. And maybe you should have a little snack before you go."

The four teammates looked at one another and smiled. They knew what that meant. It meant the Fart Squad was about to get all gassed up!

# CHAPTER FOUR

"Do you hear something?" Juan-Carlos asked as they walked along. It was after school, and the four of them had enjoyed a quick snack of the school's reheated burritos—the ones that gave them their fart powers—then changed into their uniforms and started out toward the old Bottom factory. But there were voices coming from somewhere nearby.

"Where are those masked menaces?" they heard a man demand. "How dare they steal our underwear! My butt hurts so much

I can't sit down properly, and I can barely think straight!"

"Uh-oh! We'd better hide, and fast!" Darren said. The four of them ducked into a nearby alley just as the voices grew suddenly louder. Whoever they were, they were right around the corner!

"I never trusted those kids," a second man insisted. "Hiding their faces like that—they must be up to no good!"

"And the smell!" another said. There were murmurs of agreement.

"But I can't keep going without underwear! My legs and butt are killing me!"

WHERE ARE THOSE MASKED MENACES?!

"Doesn't the department store have a warehouse down here?" someone else said. "Maybe they've still got some underwear tucked away in there!"

The group passed by the kids' alleyway, still complaining loudly. A few minutes later, their conversation had died down to a dull murmur. "Coast is clear," Juan-Carlos announced, glancing about.

"Let's go," Darren urged. "The sooner we can find the missing underwear, the better!" Juan-Carlos could see that his friend was still surprised—and hurt—that the people of Buttz-ville would be so quick to accuse the Fart Squad of this. It was upsetting for all of them.

The Bottom Factory was a big old abandoned building at the center of town, just where Stan had said it would be. It had a big rusted chain link fence around it, topped with barbed wire, but the chain on the gate

was loose enough for all of the kids, even Walter, to slip through.

"Didn't Stan say this place had shut down?" Tina asked as they approached.

"Yeah, why?" Darren asked.

"Because," Tina pointed at a window off to one side, "there's a light on in there!" Sure enough, the window was lit up from the inside.

Darren led the way to the factory and stopped right beside a grimy, dirty wall. The lit window was up at least eight feet above the ground. "Walter, do your thing," Darren said.

"Indeed," Walter replied, pulling his goggles down over his eyes, "one aerial surveillance, coming up." He took a deep breath, then let out a series of short, squeal-like farts. Then Walter began to drift up in the air, his gas lending him buoyancy like a helium balloon.

The others waited while he floated up to the window and peered inside. When Walter gave them a thumbs-up, they dragged him back down to the ground using his boots, then his cape.

"A wizened old man is within," Walter reported. "He is tinkering with some contraption and cackling to himself." Walter leaned in. "I believe I may have located the missing intimate apparel as well."

"Hey, Poindexter!" Tina shout whispered. "When're you going to drop the brainiac act already?"

"It's not an act, but rather an authentic expression of my true essence, and thus, I plan to keep it up in perpetuity...."

"Focus!" Darren clapped his hands together. "Let's get in there and find out who this old guy is and why he couldn't just buy underpants like everybody else!"

They walked along the factory wall until they spotted a small door. Tina darted ahead to try it. It was unlocked.

Stepping inside, Juan-Carlos almost choked. "Oh gross," he muttered, covering his mouth and nose with one hand. The air was thick with that same pungent fart smell from his bedroom the other morning. That explained the smell that was left behind!

But whose farts were they?

"Yeah, well, watch your step," Tina warned, narrowly avoiding a dark puddle Juan-Carlos hoped was just water. It was hard to tell for certain, since the only light was coming from that one room and the dim sunlight filtering in through the grimy windows. He could see more puddles, though, and dirt and dust were everywhere. All four of them took care to watch where they walked, their footsteps echoing off the walls as they headed toward the light.

A few minutes later, the Squad stopped to stare. They were on the factory floor now,

one enormous room with the rusty machinery still placed in rows down its length. But at the far end was a different machine, bigger and darker and newer than the rest. A little old  man darted back and forth before it, muttering to himself as he adjusted dials and knobs and buttony-type-things. Then he glanced up and saw them.

"Ah, the infamous Fart Squad," he announced, his voice sharp and wavering, but strong. "You're just in time . . . to see my greatest creation!"

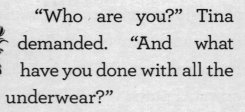

"Who are you?" Tina demanded. "And what have you done with all the underwear?"

"I? I am Doctor Lucius René Bottom," the man answered proudly. He was barely taller than Tina, with great tufts of white hair sprouting out all over his head, above his eyes, on his chin, under his nose, and even from his ears. He had on a white lab coat that had seen better days.

Juan-Carlos nudged the others. "René Bottom?" he said quietly. "Runny Bottom? Really?"

Doctor Bottom heard him. "Yes, yes," he said, frowning through his great big mustache. "Congratulations, you've hit upon the exact name my old classmates gave me when I was your age. You have no idea what it's like going through life as Runny Bottom." He gazed around them, at the rundown factory. "But that didn't stop me. I worked hard and became the Underwear King of Buttzville! 'We'll get to the Bottom of things!' was our motto, and we did! People may have still laughed at me behind my back, but I was rich and powerful!" His face twisted into a ferocious glare.

"And then the city took my company away from me and shut down my beautiful factory. I became a laughingstock again! 'Bottom hits bottom' all the papers said!" He glared at the Squad. "For years, I've wanted revenge. And after reading about that Fartasaurus, I finally realized how to get it!"

"How?" Darren asked.

"At first I foolishly thought I could replicate your powers by amassing a cache of fart gas. My children and I worked day and night to fill up silo after silo.

But as you might guess, gas is a very difficult substance to harness, and"—Bottom sighed—"our farts simply don't have the powers that yours do."

*Of course they don't,* Juan-Carlos thought. *They're missing the secret ingredient . . . radioactive bean burritos!*

"But the smell has been impossible to shake!" Bottom said.

"Well, that explains the mysterious crime scene odor!" Darren said.

Doctor Bottom nodded in agreement, then inhaled deeply and smiled, as if he were smelling a fragrant flower.

"Eventually, I realized," he continued, "that if I wanted what you had, I'd have to go directly to the source. So I stole your underwear and collected whatever remaining power I could scrape together in order to weaponize my own super-team—and now I'm using them to destroy this stupid town!" He gestured at the machine behind him, and the kids saw underwear churning about within its tubes and coils. There were bins of more underwear beside it, all wrung out like they had already been through the process.

"There are so many strange things happening in Buttzville lately," Doctor Bottom told them. "And the four of you have been right there every time. There's so much power in those farts of yours! And what do those farts have to pass through every time?" He paused, clearly waiting for them to answer.

"Underwear?" Juan-Carlos finally offered.

The doctor beamed at him. "Exactly! And if there's one thing I know, it's underwear! So by stealing yours and running it through this special extractor I built"—he patted the side of the machine fondly—"I could drain off the power, condense it, then inject it into new underwear of my own design."

"Okay, but why did you take *everybody's* underwear?" Tina demanded. "That's just cruel!"

Doctor Bottom shrugged. "I didn't know who you four really were, did I? So I just went through everybody's until I found yours!"

"But you still kept all of them," Darren pointed out. "And now people are hurting!"

"That's the best part!" Doctor Bottom laughed. "When all this is over, they'll be begging me to make them some fresh, clean underwear. But for now, they'll have to suffer, because the worst has just begun. My invention worked! I siphoned all your powers—into these!" He gestured off to the side, and the team turned—to find themselves facing four kids their own age. Each one was wearing some kind of costume with their underwear proudly displayed.

"Fart Squad," Doctor Bottom declared,

"meet the Bottom Brigade! My grandchildren," he added proudly. "I'm Jockstrap," one boy announced. He was as tall as Walter, but powerfully built where Walter was just heavy. He was wearing what looked like a wrestling uniform, but with the jockstrap on the outside.

"I'm Bikini," the only girl called out. She was tall and slender, with long dark hair pulled back in a ponytail, and she had on a bikini over her shorts and halter top.

"Thermal," said a second boy. He was small and slight and wore his underwear on his head.

"And I'm Tighty Whitey," the last boy offered. He wasn't tall or short, skinny or heavy. In fact, except for the gleaming white underwear he wore on top of his clothes, he looked completely normal. He didn't sound normal, though—he sounded slightly crazed, his voice high and fast as he laughed, and stated, "and we're going to use our new powers to make this city pay!"

"Not if we have anything to say about it," Darren replied. He turned to the others. "Fart Squad, it's time to gas things up—let's go!"

And the two teams charged toward each other, shouting and screaming and ready to fight.

# CHAPTER FIVE

Juan-Carlos darted right in front of the hulking Jockstrap. He paused and set off one of his "time-delay" farts—but before he could get away, the bigger kid grabbed him and held him easily in place, forcing Juan-Carlos to bear the brunt of his own attack. The smell was enough to make Juan-Carlos almost pass out, and a quick smack

to the head from Jock-
strap left him on the floor,
too dizzy to stand or even
speak, his vision
blurry. Score
one for the
Bottom Bri-
gade!

"You're going down!" Juan-Carlos heard
Tina shout, leaping at Bikini. But the other
girl twisted, sidestepping the attack. She was
so thin that, from the side, she completely
vanished from view! Tina paused, trying to
see where her opponent had gone, and then
reeled backward as Bikini reappeared and
punched her full in the face.

"No, you are," Bikini replied with a laugh
as Tina sprawled on the ground, unconscious. Two down.

"I shall take to the air," Walter decided,

using his farts to lift off. Thermal eyed him closely. The smaller boy didn't seem to be doing anything, really, but Walter was beginning to sweat and turn red in the face. "It is surprisingly warm up here," the largest Fart Squad member declared, fanning himself. "I am feeling light-headed." Then he fainted! Fortunately, without being awake to control them, his farts faded, too, and Walter drifted down to the factory floor.

But that was three down, and Darren was now the only Fart Squad member left standing. "Things are about to get too hot for you to handle," he warned Tighty Whitey, turning to present his butt to his rival. "Fire in the—"

But before Darren could finish his catchphrase, much less get off a fart, something long and thin wrapped itself around his arms and chest. Then something else wrapped around from the other side, and then two more things circled his legs. Darren was glancing down in confusion. Juan-Carlos was puzzled, too. There were what looked like four thick white rubber hoses coiling about his friend! What was going on here?

"Better not fart now," Tighty Whitey warned, and Darren glanced over his shoulder, surprised. The other kid was right next to him, so close they were practically hugging. No, wait, they were hugging—it was Tighty Whitey's arms and legs that were wrapped around Darren! The boy was like a human boa constrictor! "If you let that fire loose, you might explode," Darren's rival continued.

It was true—Juan-Carlos knew Darren didn't dare fart as long as he was all wrapped up. He tried to break free instead, but the other boy's limbs were too strong. And they were so tight Darren was clearly having trouble breathing. He gasped, still struggling, but Juan-Carlos could see that his friend was getting weaker. Eventually Darren went limp, all the fight drained out of him.

"Looks like our Bottoms are fart-proof!" Tighty Whitey said with a laugh as he released Darren at last, who slid to the ground, barely conscious.

The battle was over. And the Fart Squad had lost.

"Don't get in our way again," Tighty Whitey warned as he and his teammates dragged the Fart Squad over to an oversize laundry cart and dumped them in. "Or we'll do a lot more than knock you out." Then they shoved the cart out through the factory doors, spilling the Fart Squad onto the dank, dirty ground around the factory and slamming the doors shut behind them. That was all Juan-Carlos saw—the impact when he hit the ground was enough to complete what Jockstrap had started, and he passed out right afterward.

"What happened?" Tina asked when she woke up a short time later. "All I remember is that Bikini girl disappearing, and then nothing."

"She dispatched you with alacrity, I am afraid," Walter replied, groaning and levering himself up as well. "Not that I fared much better." He glanced over at Darren, who was shaking his head to clear it. "I take it from your appearance that you did not emerge victorious either?"

"No," Darren admitted glumly. "They beat the pants off all of us." It was the first time the Fart Squad had really been beaten, and it felt terrible. Especially since they'd gotten beat by a bunch of kids whose abilities were stolen from their fart powers!

"We should get out of here," Juan-Carlos suggested. "Before something worse happens." For once, he didn't even try to make a joke. None of them were finding anything very funny right now.

The kids dragged themselves up and Darren led the way out of the factory yard. They all stayed silent as they headed back into town and toward their homes, bruised, exhausted, and dejected.

Then they rounded a corner and a shout rang out. "There they are!" It was some man in a suit. "Give us back our underwear!" he demanded, racing toward the kids.

A whole group of other men and women were behind him, and they all charged the Fart Squad as well. "Yeah, we want our underwear!" the mob cried.

"We don't have them!" Darren shouted back. "We didn't take them! The Bottoms Brigade did!"

But nobody was listening.

Walter tugged on Darren's sleeve. "I suggest a hasty retreat," he said quietly.

"Yeah," Tina agreed. "Run!"

"I have a better idea," Walter offered. He held out his hands and squeezed his eyes shut, cheeks puffing out with effort. "Hold on!"

With the mob closing in, and clearly not willing to talk, the team had no choice but to grab onto Walter and let him fart them up into the air and out of harm's way. Especially since they didn't want to turn their powers on innocent people—and probably weren't up to another fight right now anyway.

So they fled. Fortunately it was dark enough that, once they'd drifted up ten feet or so, the team could disappear into the shadows. Walter used a series of smaller farts to propel them forward, and once they'd slipped around a corner and over a narrow alley, they descended again, on the next block.

"Whew, that was close!" Juan-Carlos said after they were sure they were safe. "Imagine getting flattened by the same people we keep saving—that would've really been awful!"

The others just nodded.

"Guess I'll see you guys tomorrow at school," Darren muttered when they reached the spot where they'd all split off toward their homes.

And with that, the Fart Squad members went their separate ways.

"Something got you down, son?" Mr. Finkelstein asked as he stuck his head into Juan-Carlos's room later that night. "Because if you got any lower, you'd be underground!"

Even one of his dad's jokes wasn't enough to make Juan-Carlos crack a smile this time. "Sorry, Dad," he answered. He almost told his dad what was really going on, but at the last minute managed to stop himself. He couldn't reveal the Squad's secret, not without the others' permission. The closest he could get was to say, "It's just this whole underwear thing is really getting to me." Which was true—he was so sore he could barely stand it.

"Don't worry," his father replied, as he entered the room and sat down on the bed beside Juan-Carlos. "This underwear drought won't last forever. One way or another, it's going to get fixed. Who knows, maybe the Fart Squad will take care of it."

"No, they won't!" Juan-Carlos snapped, finally sick of hearing his dad go on about the Squad. "I know you think they're the best thing since toilet paper, but they're just kids! And right now, they're kids everyone else thinks are criminals! There's nothing they can do! They can't fix everything!"

"Uh, okay, maybe not," his dad agreed, clearly surprised by Juan-Carlos's blowing up at him. "But I'm sure it'll all work out somehow, anyway." He patted his son on the arm carefully, like he was afraid touching him would set Juan-Carlos off again. "In the meantime, why don't you get some sleep?"

"Yeah. Good night, Dad." Juan-Carlos flopped back and then twisted around to bury his face in his pillow as his dad got up and left the room. Great. His dad still thought the Squad could do no wrong, but now he probably thought Juan-Carlos himself was losing it.

Could things get any worse?

# CHAPTER SIX

Apparently things *could* get worse. And did.

"No need to worry about getting up," Juan-Carlos's mom told him the next morning, peeking into his room. "School's closed."

"What? Why?" Juan-Carlos realized his mom was looking at him funny. Who ever heard of a kid complaining that he couldn't go to school? "I mean, I was looking forward to hanging out with my friends."

"Well, you could still get together with them, maybe. Rivkah's over at Jennifer's house. They issued a curfew and closed the school to keep children off the street. This way, if any of those Fart Squad kids are on the loose, they'll be easier to spot. But if there's an adult who can supervise you, that's fine. I would, but I've got my bridge club this afternoon."

Juan-Carlos reached for his glasses. "Don't worry—I know just the one," he promised.

"All right," Stan said. He'd agreed immediately to Juan-Carlos's plan, and now the five of them were gathered near the town's drive-in movie theater, where they'd trained a few times before. "Tell me what happened yesterday."

"They cleaned our clocks," Juan-Carlos

answered. "We never stood a chance."

"I need more details," their mentor insisted. "Walk me through the entire thing."

So they did— starting with reaching the Bottom Factory, then describing Doctor Bottom and his machine and then the Bottom Brigade. Finally each of them recounted what had happened when they'd fought the other team.

". . . and then he dropped me on the ground like a piece of trash," Darren finished. He shuddered, probably from the memory of those arms and legs wrapped around him like snakes. "I didn't even get off a shot."

"Me neither," Tina agreed.

"I was defeated with ease," Walter offered.

Juan-Carlos just nodded.

"All right." Stan stroked his chin. "You were at a disadvantage that time. You guys are practically celebrities, so they'd heard about you and what you could do. But you didn't know anything about them. Now you do. So think about who they are, what they can do, and how you can stop them."

The kids frowned. "I don't see how knowing what they can do is going to help any," Juan-Carlos complained. "Jockstrap is still way too strong for me!"

"And Bikini can disappear—I can't knock her out if I can't find her!" Tina agreed.

"Thermal was able to make me overheat from a distance," Walter added. "No matter how high I float, he can still bring me down."

"We're letting them control the battle," Darren said slowly, clearly thinking it through. "We need to catch them off guard. We've got to lure them out into the open, to some place we pick, so that we can be there waiting for them."

Which got Juan-Carlos thinking . . .

# CHAPTER SEVEN

Juan-Carlos was at home later that afternoon, watching TV by himself while his mom and Rivkah were still out and his dad was in his studio prepping for the next show. "This just in!" Windy McGee announced, interrupting *Puss & Toots,* Juan-Carlos's favorite cartoon, with a breaking news report. "We've had reports that an anonymous donor has taken pity on Buttsville in its time of need and is sending an emergency shipment of underwear to help us out. This shipment is set to arrive by train at eight tomorrow night, and officials promise that they will distribute the underwear on an as-needed basis as early as Saturday morning."

This was all thanks to Juan-Carlos. He'd called this story in from a pay phone at the drive-in. His father often talked about how people calling in with tips made for a great show. Windy McGee was an  anchorwoman on TV, but there were a lot of similarities between what she did and what Mr. Finkelstein did. They were both always on the lookout for a good story.

"Just in time, too," the reporter continued,

"Buttzville Hospital says it's been overrun with cases of rug burn and similar abrasions, and every available ounce of burn cream, ointment, and topical painkiller has been used up. If we don't get some underwear soon, people will be in too much pain to even move!

*That should do the trick,* Juan-Carlos thought as he listened. *There's no way the Bottom Brigade will let the town get fresh underwear. They'll have to show up to stop that train! And we'll be waiting for them!*

But his thoughts were interrupted by a knock at the front door. Curious, Juan-Carlos limped over to answer it. It was Stan! And the rest of the Squad was right behind him!

"We've got another problem," the janitor whispered as Juan-Carlos ushered them all inside and shut the door behind them. "The school's not just closed, it's been locked down completely. Even I can't get inside. And if I can't get in there—"

"We don't have any burritos," Juan-Carlos finished for him. "Oh. Wow." Without those burritos, they were powerless! What were they going to do?

"There might be a way," Darren offered. He looked at Juan-Carlos. "But it's all on you. And your dad."

Juan-Carlos gulped. Already he didn't like the direction this plan was taking. "What do you need?" he asked slowly.

"Your dad's got a lot of influence," Stan answered. "People listen to him. Have him talk about how important it is that school be reopened. If they take the chains off and the guards away, I can get back in and get those burritos."

"Ah. Okay." That made sense. Deep down Juan-Carlos didn't really feel like giving his father yet another reason to worship the Fart Squad, but he couldn't let his jealousy get in the way of everyone's well-being.

Especially once he reminded himself that the person he was jealous of was none other than his own darn self!

The others were anxiously waiting for Juan-Carlos to answer. This wasn't just about him and his dad. It wasn't even about the Fart Squad. This was about so much more than that.

This was about the people of Buttzville.

About people everywhere.

And that's what the Fart Squad was all about.

Because, as their great scent-sei, Janitor Stan, had famously said:

"From great farts come mighty winds."

"Yeah," Juan-Carlos said finally, because he knew it was the only thing he could say. "Sure. I'll do it."

"Great!" Darren slapped him on the back. "We'll get out of here—don't want him getting suspicious." They all turned to go.

"I'll let you know as soon as I have the stash," Stan promised just before he left.

"Okay. Thanks." Juan-Carlos shut the door behind them, then leaned against it with a sigh. *Great.*

But that night, when it was time to talk to his dad, Juan-Carlos couldn't get the words out. He scarfed down his dinner and headed straight to his bedroom.

✷ ✷ ✷

"Have you talked to your dad yet?" Darren asked over the phone the next day.

"No, I haven't had a chance," Juan-Carlos lied. "He's been super busy." Which was a little true, but not really.

"Well, we're running out of time," Darren reminded him. "That train is supposed to get in tonight, remember?"

"I know. I'll talk to him," Juan-Carlos promised. But he wasn't sure if that was true or not.

✷ ✷ ✷

"Feeling any better?" Mr. Finkelstein asked Juan-Carlos that afternoon as they sat down to a late lunch of sandwiches and potato chips. Juan-Carlos's mother had taken Rivkah shopping, so the Finkelstein men had to fend for themselves.

Juan-Carlos shrugged. "I guess." He sighed.

"That's okay. I guess we're all a little out of sorts these days." His dad winked at him. "And out of shorts, too!"

Juan-Carlos couldn't help smiling a little at that one.

"Dad," he said after a second, "do you think they'll reopen the school soon?"

His father looked at him funny. "Why? Are you that eager to go back?"

"I like school," Juan-Carlos answered, then quickly corrected himself. "Well, okay, not class itself, maybe, but my friends and stuff. And it's important, right?"

"It is," his father agreed, nodding. "And

it's ridiculous that they closed school at all. This whole thing with the underwear and the Fart Squad and everything else, it's got everybody acting crazy."

"Right?" Juan-Carlos asked. So far, everything was going exactly according to plan. "Because, if *anyone* can turn this thing around"—he hesitated, *so* wishing he could just reveal his masked alter ego's identity— "it's probably the Fart Squad!"

Dad nodded. "Of course! These haters, they're just shooting themselves in the foot—or, in this case, the butt!—and making things worse for everyone!"

"Well then, Dad . . . I mean, I don't know how much my opinion counts, but—"

In an instant, his dad's expression went from excited to distressed. "Son!" He got up and came around the table, gently lifting Juan-Carlos's chin so they could see eye to eye. "Don't *ever* say that. Your opinion always counts with me, Juan-Carlos. *Always*."

Juan-Carlos believed him. But he had to ask: "Even though I'm not a superhero?"

"Hey!" His dad threw his arms around Juan-Carlos and engulfed him in a big hug. "No trash-talking yourself here, okay? You may not be a superhero, but you'll always be super to me."

Juan-Carlos relaxed into the hug. Why had he been so stupid? Of course his dad loved him! So what if he thought the Fart Squad was awesome? They *were* awesome! But that was just professional admiration. This was real.

After a minute, they finally broke apart. "You were saying . . . ?" his dad said.

"Oh, yeah—I just think it might be time for you to hit the airwaves and tell people enough is enough. . . . And that, instead of fearing the Fart Squad, they should let the Fart Squad do their thing, because . . ."

"Because they could be our last, best hope." He might have gone a little overboard with that last one, but it seemed to do the trick.

"Great idea! Don't know why I didn't think of it myself! I'm on it!" his dad said, and he headed straight to his studio.

# CHAPTER EIGHT

"Listen up, people," Mr. Finkelstein said over the radio a little while later, as Juan-Carlos listened in from upstairs. "Everybody's sore right now—in more ways than one!—and we're all looking for someone to blame. Maybe the Fart Squad had something to do with all this, and maybe they didn't, but shutting down school isn't the answer. Our children need to learn!

"Remember people," Juan-Carlos's dad added. "It's still 'innocent until proven guilty' here in America, last time I checked.

No sense raising a stink over nothing!" Juan-Carlos grinned as he clicked off the radio. What his dad said had been perfect! Now they just had to hope enough people listened and agreed with him.

✿ ✿ ✿

"You did it!" Tina said that night as Juan-Carlos met up with the others by the school.

"My dad did," Juan-Carlos answered proudly. "But yeah."

Just as they'd hoped, Mr. Finkelstein's listeners had swamped City Hall with phone calls until the mayor finally relented. The guards and chains went away, the school was opened soon after, and children were no longer restricted in their activities. Regular classes would start up again on Monday. The four of them had wasted no time telling their parents about a last-minute stargazing assignment they had to complete, and fleeing their homes before their parents could ask too many questions. Now they were gathered here, waiting for the next step in their plan.

"Here we go, kids," Stan declared, emerging from the school. "Now that I can get into my closet again, it's no problem to get my

hands on these bad boys!" He carried a familiar Tupperware container in his hands, and the kids cheered. He'd brought out the burritos!

✵ ✵ ✵

Twenty minutes later, gassed up and ready to go, the Squad said good-bye to Stan—who had an errand of his own to perform—and set out for the Buttzville train station. It was a beautiful old building right in the heart of town, just to one side of the center square, which made it easy to get from one place to anywhere else. Unfortunately, that also meant it was easy to see people coming or going. Like the cops who were lined up outside.

"Poop!" Tina muttered as they crouched behind some bushes next to a building across the street. "How're we going to get in there without the cops seeing us? And possibly arresting us?"

Walter gulped. "I hope we can avoid that," he said softly, looking a little green in the face. "Incarceration is not high on my list

of evening activities, and could jeopardize some of my plans for the future."

"Nobody's arresting us," Darren assured them. "We're just four ordinary kids out for a late-night stroll around the train station. That's all."

"Yeah, until they check our bags and find our uniforms," Juan-Carlos pointed out. "What then?"

"Oh. Right." Darren looked at the train station, then at the cops surrounding it. He scanned the trees and bushes and then he looked up.

"I think I know a way to get us in without them stopping us," he said finally. He grinned at the rest of them. "We're just going to give them something they won't expect."

Twenty minutes later, Tina was doing her best not to shout or kick. Or punch—punching would have been a really bad idea right now—since she was hanging by her arms. At least a hundred feet above the ground.

"If you drop me," she warned in a whisper, "I'm going to murder you."

"Although that makes little sense, your concern is noted," Walter replied just as quietly. "I will not drop you. You are perfectly safe."

She clearly didn't feel safe, though, as the four of them floated across the street. They'd climbed up to the top of the

building facing the train station to avoid
being seen, and then Walter had lifted off.
Once he was airborne, he had grabbed
Tina's arms, and Juan-Carlos and Darren
had each grabbed one of his legs. The cops
would never notice because they weren't
likely to think of looking up.

At least, that's what the kids were hoping.

But apparently Darren had been right,
because they made it across to the train
station without any problem. The building

had a sharply sloped red-tile roof with windows jutting out at intervals, and it was easy enough for the four of them to float up to one of those windows and slip inside. Then they made their way down to the ground floor.

"You see?" Walter said to Tina. "I did not drop you once."

"Well, let's not make a habit of traveling this way," she replied. Then she handed over the duffel bags she'd slung over her shoulders. "Here."

"Thanks." Darren grinned as he took his. "Okay, let's do this!"

The four of them ducked into the bathrooms. A few minutes later, the Fart Squad was back and ready for action!

"You really think they're going to go after the train?" Juan-Carlos asked Darren as they crept across the station toward the platforms. Some stations had their platforms outside and only the waiting rooms, restrooms, and ticket offices inside, but the Buttzville station was large enough and grand enough for the platforms themselves to be within the building.

"Absolutely," Darren answered. "But they'll wait until it's pulled in and the underwear's been taken off. Why unload it yourself when you can have somebody else do it for you?"

"There're police everywhere, though," Tina pointed out. "If Stan doesn't come through, we won't be able to risk it." Stan had promised he would scatter the cops so that they wouldn't get hurt.

"He'll take care of it," Darren assured her, even

though he looked like he was worrying about the same thing.

But a minute or two before eight, all of the cops' walkie-talkies started going nuts. "We've got a possible break-in at the mayor's," the kids heard from where they were hiding behind a couple of columns. "All units, respond ASAP."

"Everybody, let's go!" a police captain shouted. "Double-time!"

"But, sir," one of the officers dared to ask as there was a mad dash for the doors, "what about the train? What about the under-wear?"

"We'll get back as soon as we can,"

his captain answered. "This is the mayor, man! Now get a move on!"

"What do you think Stan did?" Juan-Carlos wondered aloud as the four of them emerged from their hiding place a few minutes later. They had the train station all to themselves.

Tina shrugged. "Tossed a brick through the front window. Set off the mayor's car alarm. Triggered the sprinklers on the front lawn. TPed his house. Left a stink bomb on the front porch." She realized that her teammates were all staring at her, and shrugged again. "What? I may have given Stan a few ideas."

"Whatever it was, it definitely worked," Darren commented, spinning around in a circle, his arms stretched out wide to the sides. "We've got the whole place to ourselves!"

"Which just means there isn't anybody here to watch you get beat down a second time," someone called out from down toward the station's far end. "Which is a real shame."

Juan-Carlos looked up. It was them! The Bottom Brigade had taken the bait!

He grinned as he and his teammates

clustered together and walked to meet their rivals. "Oh, it's going to be a shame, all right," he replied loud enough for them to hear. "But we aren't going to be the ones ashamed."

Beside him, the others nodded, even though it had been a lame comeback. Still, it got the point across. But inside, Juan-Carlos felt a twinge of worry. Could they really beat their rivals—or was the Fart Squad about to get spanked again?

# CHAPTER NINE

"Okay, Squad, time to gas up!" Darren shouted.

"Yeah!" Tina agreed, smacking her fists together.

"We'll get to the *bottom* of this!" Juan-Carlos joked, causing the others to groan. But at least he was feeling positive enough to make terrible jokes again!

"Oh, yes, the long-anticipated rematch," Walter added. He chuckled ominously. "And this time the outcome will be decidedly different." And with that, and a series of small but potent toots, Walter took to the air.

"Not so fast, big guy," Thermal snapped, stepping forward and glaring up at Walter. But before he could do anything more than look, Darren was in the Brigade member's face.

"So you want to turn up the heat?" Darren demanded. "Fine!" He spun about and let off a fiery fart that made Thermal yelp and jump to the side. "Let's see if you can handle it—or if you burn!"

Jockstrap grinned and raised a meaty fist as he lumbered toward Juan-Carlos.

"Remember me, shrimp?"

"Unfortunately, yes," Juan-Carlos replied. "But do you remember—*her*?" And he stepped to one side, revealing Tina, who had been standing quietly right behind him.

The sight of a tiny little girl, all big eyes and a pouty smile, standing right in his way stopped Jockstrap in his tracks. Then there was suddenly an overpoweringly foul odor, and the mightiest Bottom gasped, his eyes rolling up in his head, as he collapsed. He hit the ground like a bag of beans, and was out cold.

"No!" Bikini shrieked. "I'll get you for that, you little—" But stopped when Juan-Carlos got between her and Tina.

"If you want her, you're going to have to go through me," he declared, trying to sound a lot braver than he felt.

"With pleasure," Bikini snarled. She turned to the side, disappearing from view, and Juan-Carlos gulped and ran. He headed straight down the middle of the station, not bothering to duck or dodge. It would have looked, to anybody watching, like he was running from nothing at all . . .

. . . until there was a small cry and a girl suddenly appeared, stumbling as she choked and tried to breathe.

"I don't need to see you to know you're coming after me," Juan-Carlos explained, turning to face the gasping girl. "And my time bombs can hit you whether you're visible or not."

"But now you're right there in plain sight," Tina said sweetly, stepping up beside the still-woozy Bikini. "Which means you're easy pickings." A sudden burst of stench, and Tina smiled as her rival fell over, unconscious.

"No!" Tighty Whitey yelled as he saw his teammates fall. "This can't be happening! We had you beat last time!"

"Last time we allowed you to dictate the terms of our engagement," a voice called down from above. Tighty Whitey glanced up to find Walter hovering directly above him. "This time, we control the field." He held up a brick he'd collected earlier that night on their way to the station. "Bombs away!" Walter declared as he dropped the brick right at Tighty Whitey's head.

"Ha, is that the best you've got?!" the Bottom Brigade's leader taunted as he sidestepped the falling missile. "You think

you're out of reach up there? Think again!"
And he lunged upward, his arms shooting
up like airborne streamers, extending farther and farther as his hands groped for the
flying Fart Squad member.

"Ah, perhaps more altitude is required,"
Walter muttered, trying to fart again for
added lift. But it was too late—Tighty Whitey's hands had found him! They grabbed
onto Walter's sweatshirt and then continued
to circle him, wrapping him in extendable
arms and dragging him back to the ground.

"Got you!" Tighty Whitey crowed. "Now
who's in control?"

But, much to his sur-
prise, Walter smiled. "As
a matter of fact, I am,"
he called back while
deliberately holding in
an impending fart. The

trapped gas caused him to expand even more, becoming rounder and more blimplike.

And causing Tighty Whitey's arms to stretch even farther to cover Walter's increasing bulk.

"Stop!" Tighty Whitey shouted, struggling to hold on. Sweat had broken out on his face. "Please!"

"I think not," Walter replied, still expanding. He drifted higher, dragging Tighty Whitey's hands with him and forcing the Bottom to stretch even more or else get dragged up into the air himself.

Now Tighty Whitey was sweating profusely, and his face was twisted with agony. "Can't . . . hold . . . on . . . much longer," he gasped. Then he shuddered, his eyes rolled back, and he collapsed, his arms contracting back down to normal size, now that he was unconscious.

That left only one. Thermal. He and Darren were engaged in a duel, fighting fire with fire. While Thermal's game was to make his opponent overheat, Darren's was to release all his heat through his burning farts, which were now scorching Thermal in return. And though he could increase heat in others, Thermal himself apparently wasn't very good at handling it. After a particularly foul and fiery fart from Darren, Thermal dropped to his knees.

"Please, no more!" he begged. "I give up!"

"Tell us what your grandfather did with the rest of the town's underwear!" Darren demanded over his shoulder, keeping his butt at the ready in case Thermal was trying to trick him.

But the Bottom didn't have any fight left. "It's all still at the factory," he admitted with a shudder. "Grandpa didn't need the underwear anymore after giving us our powers, so he kept them just to hurt everybody else."

"That fiend!" a voice called out. Darren and the others looked around. It was that reporter for the *Buttzville Nightly News*, Windy McGee, the same one who'd been bad-mouthing the Squad. But now she was glaring at the Bottom Brigade instead. "I heard the whole thing," she assured the Squad. She gestured to the cameraman standing beside her. "Now I know who's really to blame for all this! And I have their confession on tape!"

"So you're going to stop saying mean things about us on TV?" Tina demanded, giving McGee a hard stare.

"Absolutely!" the reporter promised. "I'm going to go on right now and report what happened here, and show everyone how the Fart Squad has saved us—again."

Darren nodded. "Good. And tell them that the missing underwear is at the old Bottom factory. We're heading over now."

"You got it," McGee said. "I'll make my live report, then catch up."

The Fart Squad left the reporter there, along with the Bottom Brigade. Apparently admitting to everything had been too much for Thermal—he had collapsed with his teammates. As the Fart Squad left, the police were coming back in to arrest the Brigade. Apparently word spread fast because none of them gave the costumed quartet a hard time. A few cops even nodded as the kids ran by. One older policeman saluted.

"Nice not being a wanted criminal," Tina commented as they raced from the train station, toward the old factory.

"Yeah, I'd say we got our rep back—by the seat of our pants," Juan-Carlos offered. His friends sighed, but Juan-Carlos just grinned. He was back!

"Now let's go get that underwear," Darren reminded the others. "And Doctor Bottom."

# CHAPTER TEN

But when the kids reached the factory, Doctor Bottom was ready for them.

"I may not have any powered undies left," he declared, "but I can still pants you kids!" He lifted what looked like a bazooka made from the same tubing as the power-draining machine. A long tube connected it to one of the bins behind him.

"What're you gonna do, shoot dirty undies at us?" Juan-Carlos asked with a laugh.

"Something like that," the old man agreed with a nasty grin. He set the weapon on his narrow shoulder, aimed it at them, and pulled the trigger. A wadded-up ball of underwear shot out and slammed Juan-Carlos in the chest, hard enough to knock him back a step.

"Hey, that hurt!" he yelped, rubbing at his chest. That was going to leave a bruise!

"That's the idea!" Doctor Bottom said, cackling. He flipped a switch on the weapon. "And now, full auto!"

"Look out!" Darren shouted as a whole stream of wadded-up underwear shot out toward the Squad. He tried turning his flaming farts on the cotton missiles, but only succeeded in lighting them on fire. "Yikes! Sorry!"

There wasn't time for Walter to float up out of harm's way, much less grab the rest of them. Instead the kids all dove for cover behind some of the old bins scattered nearby. The barrage didn't last very long, and a minute later they cautiously stuck their heads out to look around.

The mad doctor had vanished. Only the empty undie-gun remained.

"He's gone!" Darren said, jumping to his feet. "Darn it!" He kicked one of the bins in frustration.

"Who's gone?" Windy McGee asked as she stepped into the warehouse. "Doctor Bottom?"

The kids nodded.

"That's too bad. I really wanted to ask him a few questions. Wow, what is that awful smell?"

"Well, if one of those questions was 'Where's our underwear?' I think we already have an answer," Darren said, pointing toward where Doctor Bottom had just been standing. There was the same large machine he had used to consolidate the energy from the Squad's farts and then transfer that power to the Bottom Brigade, and beside it were several rows of large bins, filled with underpants both clean and used.

"Yes!" the reporter declared. She turned to face her cameraman, and started to report about the situation: "This is Windy McGee with breaking news! The heroes known as the Fart Squad have recovered Buttzville's

missing underwear! They . . ."

"We did it, gang!" Darren told the others, exchanging high fives and backslaps with his three friends. "We stopped them and recovered the underwear!"

"I wish we'd been able to nab Doctor Bottom too, though," Tina said as the four of them snuck away, changed back into their regular clothes, and then returned to watch from the shadows as McGee delivered her report.

"The police may yet apprehend him, now that they know to look," Walter commented.

"Yeah," Juan-Carlos added, "he's bound to hit rock *bottom* at this rate!"

The others sighed, and he chuckled. "That was a good one," Juan-Carlos said to himself. "Wait until I tell Dad!"

It *was* good, they all agreed, watching the news reporter clear their names and chatting and joking and laughing again. Sure, Doctor Bottom was still out there, and might come after them again, but Juan-Carlos wasn't too worried. For now he just wanted to enjoy the fact that they'd succeeded. They had their reputation back, and their confidence. And, most important of all, their underwear!

"I can't wait to get into a clean pair of undies," Juan-Carlos told the rest of them. "I'm going to leave 'going commando' to the soldiers!"

"It'll be great having underwear again," Darren agreed. "And people knowing the Fart Squad are heroes is even better."

And the four of them cheered as they sat and watched more and more grown-ups arrive to help get Buttzville's underwear back where it belonged. The town's butts would soon be covered again—thanks to the Fart Squad.

THE END

"Wakey, wakey, Mr. Stonkadopolis," a voice whispered.

Darren Stonkadopolis could hardly open his eyes. "Who's that?" he mumbled, before reaching down his pants to scratch himself. He scratched and scratched and furiously scratched some more, but instead of calming the raging itch in his butt, he only made things worse.

"It is I, Harold Buttz, *Senior*. Owner of the Buttz Factory, Buttz Industries, Buttz Bakery, Buttz Office Supply, Buttz Savings and Loan, and two-thirds of everything else in Buttzville. Now WAKE UP, son! We've no time to waste!"

Darren's eyes popped wide open. "Whoa!" he shouted, realizing Harold Buttz's face was hovering only an inch from his own. There was just enough light to make out his super-thick sideburns and black fedora hat, with a long turquoise peacock feather sticking out from the side.

*Where am I?* Darren wondered. *And what's Harold Buttz, the richest man in all of Buttzville, doing here?*

Darren quickly got up from the cot he'd been lying on. Now he could see that the rest of the Squad was asleep in the cots next to his. But how did they all get there in the first place?

"I must apologize for my men's slightly aggressive tactics," Mr. Buttz said.

With that, the nightmarish details of the last twelve hours all came flooding back to Darren. The army of scary-looking men in black suits and sunglasses sneaking up on them. The frenzied, fart-powered retaliation. And finally, a stabbing feeling that came from behind and then: darkness.

"*Slightly?*" Darren squawked. "They took us down with tranquilizer darts!"

"Well, that's why I'm apologizing!" Buttz barked. "But I had to ensure your arrival by any means necessary. I need you and your friends to complete the most important mission in the history of Buttzville."

"Mission?" Darren was still a little woozy. "What kind of mission? And how do you know who I am, anyway?"

"How do I know?" Mr. Buttz snorted. "I'm Harold R. Buttz, son. I know everything."

"Dude . . ." Juan-Carlos Finkelstein sat up drowsily in his cot. "Where are we?" Normally, he would have chimed in with a bad joke, but he was focused on relieving his own raging itch by dragging himself across the floor in a seated position, like a Chihuahua that had just eaten chili.

"I, too, am baffled by this dim and

unfamiliar location," Walter Turnip, the heaviest and most well-spoken Fart Squad member, added as he raked his behind with the fork he kept with him at all times in case of unexpected food opportunities.

"This is all so inappropriate." Tina Heiney sighed. She may have looked like an adorable little princess, but the stink of her silent-but-deadly farts was lethal.

"Linda!" Mr. Buttz shouted into the darkness. "Our young heroes are finally awake. Lights on!"

A loud *ker-chunk* echoed overhead, as blinding floodlights suddenly whirred to life.

Shielding his eyes from the bright lights, Darren looked around, and his mind was officially blown.